THE WISE OLD WOMAN

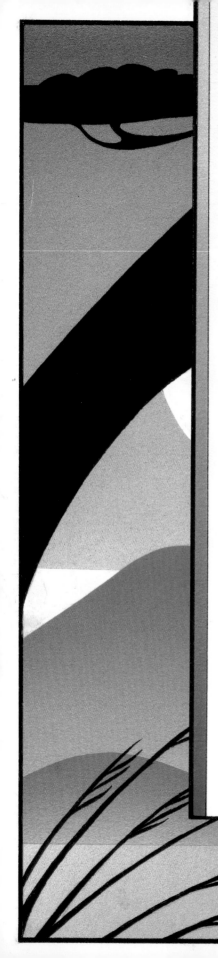

Also by Yoshiko Uchida

Journey Home
illustrated by Charles Robinson
A Jar of Dreams
The Best Bad Thing
The Happiest Ending
The Magic Purse
illustrated by Keiko Narahashi

(MARGARET K. McELDERRY BOOKS)

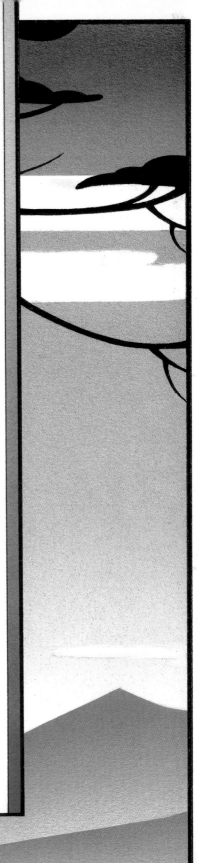

THE
WISE OLD
WOMAN

retold by
Yoshiko Uchida

illustrated by
Martin Springett

MARGARET K. McELDERRY BOOKS
New York

Maxwell Macmillan Canada
Toronto

Maxwell Macmillan International
New York   Oxford   Singapore   Sydney

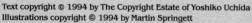

Margaret K. McElderry Books   Maxwell Macmillan Canada, Inc.
Macmillan Publishing Company   1200 Eglinton Avenue East
866 Third Avenue   Suite 200
New York, NY 10022   Don Mills, Ontario M3C 3N1

Macmillan Publishing Company is part of the Maxwell Communication
Group of Companies.
First edition
Printed in Hong Kong by South China Printing Company (1988) Ltd.
10 9 8 7 6 5 4 3 2 1
The text of this book is set in 14-point Benguiat Book.
The illustrations are rendered in airbrush and ink.

Library of Congress Cataloging-in-Publication Data
Uchida, Yoshiko.
    The wise old woman / retold by Yoshiko Uchida ; illustrated by Martin
Springett. — 1st ed.
        p.   cm.
        Summary: An old woman demonstrates the value of her age when
she solves a warlord's three riddles and saves her village from
destruction.
        ISBN 0-689-50582-5
        [1. Folklore—Japan.   2. Old age—Folklore.]   I. Springett, Martin, ill.
II. Title.
PZ8.1.U35Wi 1994   [398.21]—dc20   92-46048

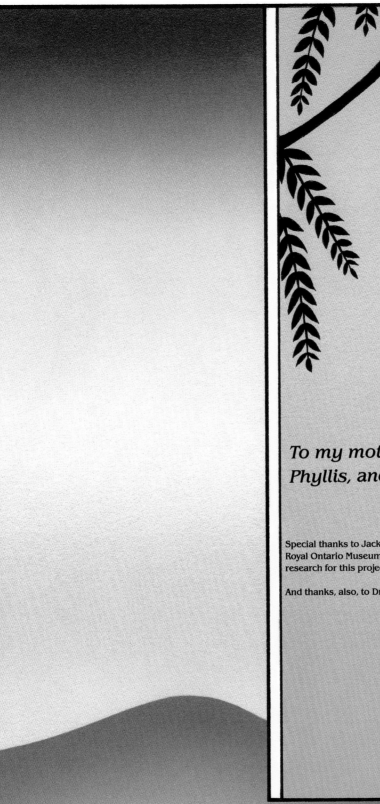

To my mother, Joan, mother-in-law, Phyllis, and aunt Kathleen

Special thanks to Jack Howard and Hugh Wylie of the Far Eastern Library, Royal Ontario Museum, for their knowledgeable assistance during the research for this project.

And thanks, also, to Dr. Marjorie Wani.

—M.S.

ong ago in the wooded hills of Japan, a young farmer and his aged mother lived in a village ruled by a cruel young lord.

"Anyone over seventy is no longer useful," the lord declared, "and must be taken into the mountains and left to die."

When the young farmer's mother reached the dreaded age, he could not bear to think of what he must do. But his mother spoke the words he could not say.

"It is time now for you to take me into the mountains," she said softly.

So, early the next morning, the farmer lifted his mother to his back and reluctantly set off up the steep mountain path.

p and up he climbed—until the trees hid the sun, and the path was gone, until he could no longer hear the birds, but only the sound of the wind shivering through the trees.

On and on he climbed. But soon he heard his mother breaking off small twigs from the trees they passed.

"I'm marking the path for you, my son," she said, "so you will not lose your way going home."

The young farmer could bear it no longer.

other, I cannot leave you behind in the mountains," he said. "We are going home together, and I will never, ever leave you."

And so, in the dark shadows of night, the farmer carried his mother back home. He dug a deep cave beneath the kitchen, and from that day, the old woman lived in this secret room, spinning and weaving. In this way two years passed, and no one in the village knew of the farmer's secret.

Then one day, three fierce warriors in full armor galloped into the small village like a sudden mountain storm.

"We come from the mighty Lord Higa to warn you," they shouted to the young lord. "When three suns have set and three moons have risen, he will come to conquer your village."

T he cruel young lord was not very brave. "Please,"
he begged, "I will do anything if you will spare me."

"Lord Higa knows no mercy," the warriors thundered, "but he
does respect a clever mind. Solve the three impossible tasks
written upon this scroll and you and your village will be saved."

Then, tossing the scroll at the young lord, they galloped off as
quickly as they had come.

F irst, make a coil of rope out of ashes," the young lord read. "Second, run a single thread through the length of a crooked log. And third, make a drum that sounds without being beaten."

The young lord quickly gathered the six wisest people of his village and ordered them to solve the impossible tasks. They put their heads together and pondered through the night. But when the stars had vanished and the roosters began to crow, they still had no answers for the young lord.

They hurried to the village shrine and sounded the giant bronze bell. "Help us," they pleaded to the gods. But the gods remained silent.

hey went next to seek the clever badger of the forest, for they knew that animals are sometimes wiser than men.

"Surely, you can help us," they said eagerly.

But the badger only shook his head. "As clever as I am," he said, "I see no way to solve such impossible tasks as these."

When the six wise people returned to the young lord without any answers, he exploded in anger.

"You are all stupid fools!" he shouted, and he threw them into his darkest dungeon. Then he posted a sign in the village square offering a bag of gold to anyone who could help him.

he young farmer hurried home to tell his mother about the impossible tasks and Lord Higa's threat. "What are we to do?" he asked sadly. "We will soon be conquered by yet another cruel lord."

The old woman thought carefully and then asked her son to bring her a coil of rope, a crooked log with a hole running through the length of it, and a small hand drum. When the farmer had done as she asked, she set to work.

First, she soaked the coil of rope in salt water and dried it well. Then, setting a match to it, she let it burn. But it did not crumble. It held its shape.

"There," she said. "This is your rope of ash."

Next she put a little honey at one end of the crooked log, and at the other, she placed an ant with a silk thread tied to it. The farmer watched in amazement as the tiny ant wound its way through the hole to get to the honey, taking the silk thread with it. And the second task was done.

Finally, the old woman opened one side of the small hand drum and sealed a bumblebee inside. As the bee beat itself against the sides of the drum trying to escape, the drum sounded without being beaten. And the third task was done.

hen the farmer presented the three completed tasks to the young lord, he was astonished. "Surely a young man such as you could not be wiser than the wisest people of our village," he said. "Tell me, what person of wisdom helped you solve these impossible tasks?"

The young farmer could not lie, and he told the lord how he had kept his mother hidden for the past two years. "It is she who solved each of your tasks and saved our village from Lord Higa," he explained.

The farmer waited to be thrown into the dungeon for disobeying the lord. But instead of being angry, the young lord was silent and thoughtful.

I have been wrong," he said at last. "Never again will I send our old people into the mountains to die. Henceforth they will be treated with respect and honor, and will share with us the wisdom of their years."

Whereupon the young lord freed everyone in his dungeon. Next he summoned the old woman and gave her three bags of gold for saving the village.

Finally he allowed the farmer to march with his finest warriors to Lord Higa's castle.

The long procession wound slowly over the mountain roads carrying its precious cargo. And it was the young farmer who carried the lord's banner fluttering high in the autumn wind.

hen they presented to Lord Higa the rope of ash and the threaded log and the drum that sounded without being beaten, he stroked his chin thoughtfully.

"I see there is much wisdom in your small village," he said, "for you have solved three truly impossible tasks. Go home," he directed the young farmer, "and tell your lord that his people deserve to live in peace."

From that day on, Lord Higa never threatened the small village again. The villagers prospered, and the young farmer and his mother lived in peace and plenty for all the days of their lives.